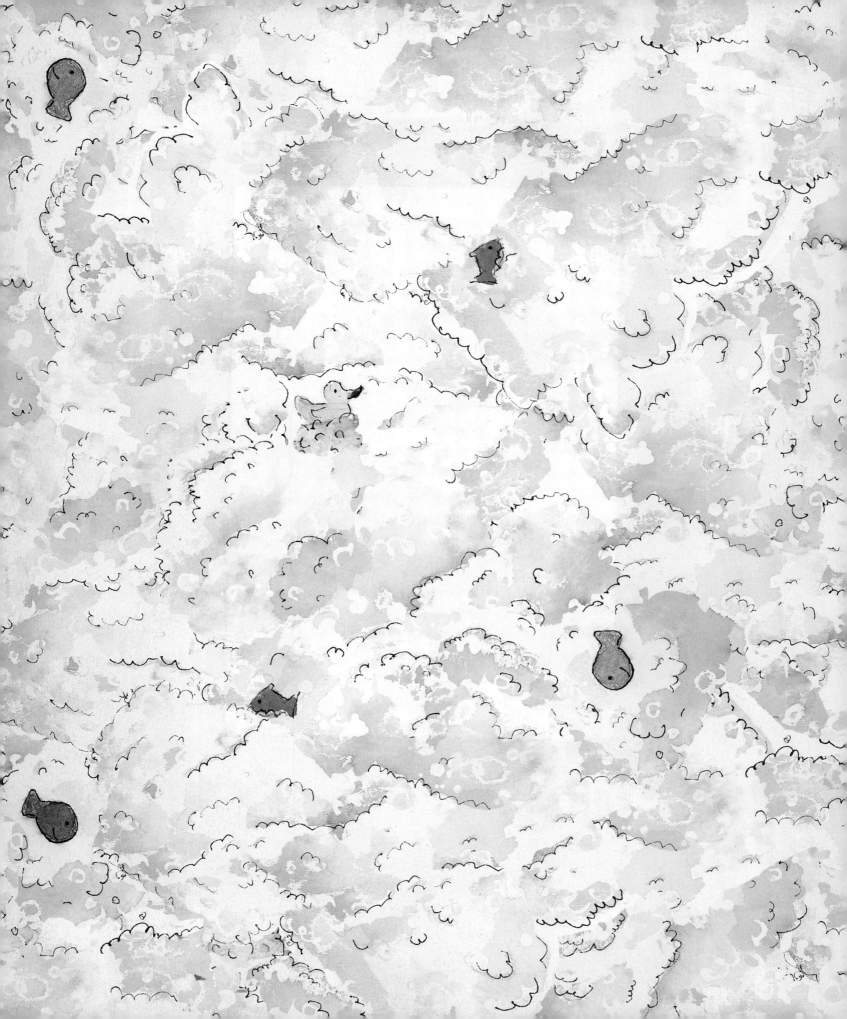

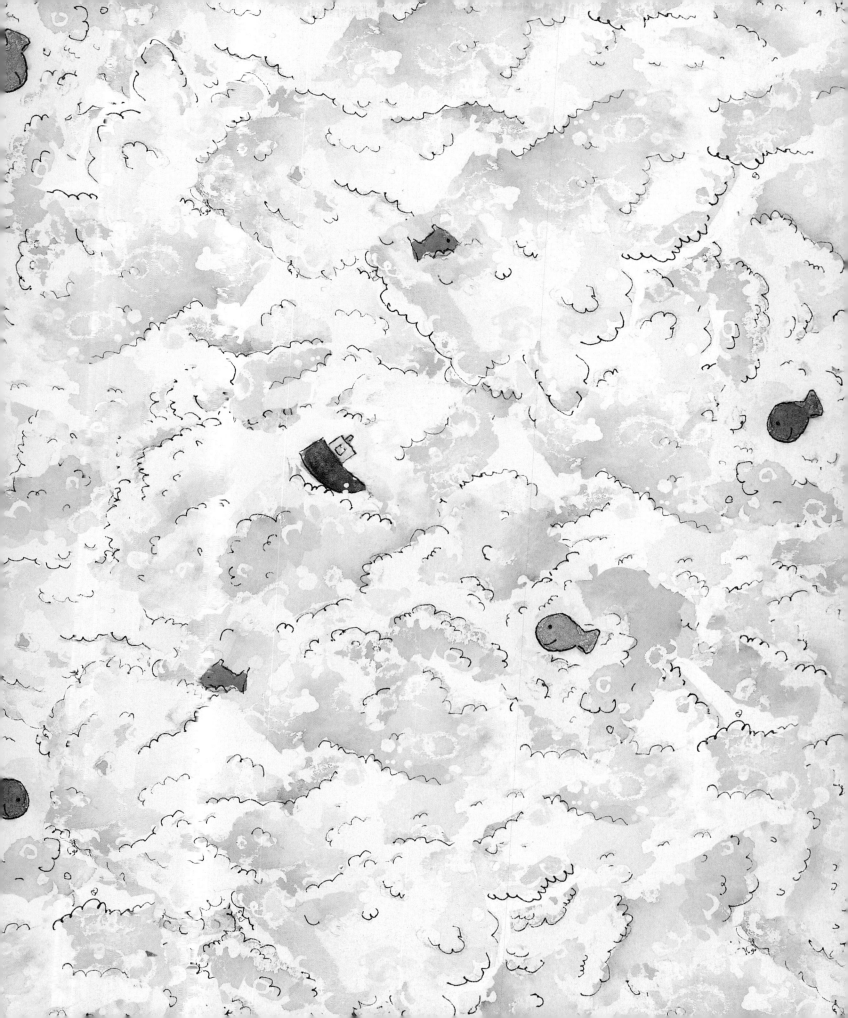

A Little Bit

Written by
Christine & Peter Maniaty

Illustrated by
Claire Richards

■ SCHOLASTIC

For Liam, Aidan and Ryan, great little guys –
CM & PM

For Ruth –
CR

First published in 2008 by Scholastic Australia
First published in the UK in 2009 by Scholastic Children's Books
Euston House, 24 Eversholt Street
London NW1 1DB
a division of Scholastic Ltd
www.scholastic.co.uk
London ~ New York ~ Toronto ~ Sydney ~ Auckland
Mexico City ~ New Delhi ~ Hong Kong

978 1407 11167 4

1 3 5 7 9 10 8 6 4 2

I'm a little bit big

and a little bit small.

A little bit short

and a little bit tall.

A little bit happy

and a little bit sad.

A little bit good

and a little bit bad.

A little bit messy

and a little bit clean.

A little bit kind

and a little bit mean.

A little bit slow

and a little bit fast.

A little bit first

and a little bit last.

A little bit scary

and a little bit funny.

A little bit gloomy

and a little bit sunny.

A little bit serious

and a little bit fun.

I'm a little bit of everything
all rolled into one.

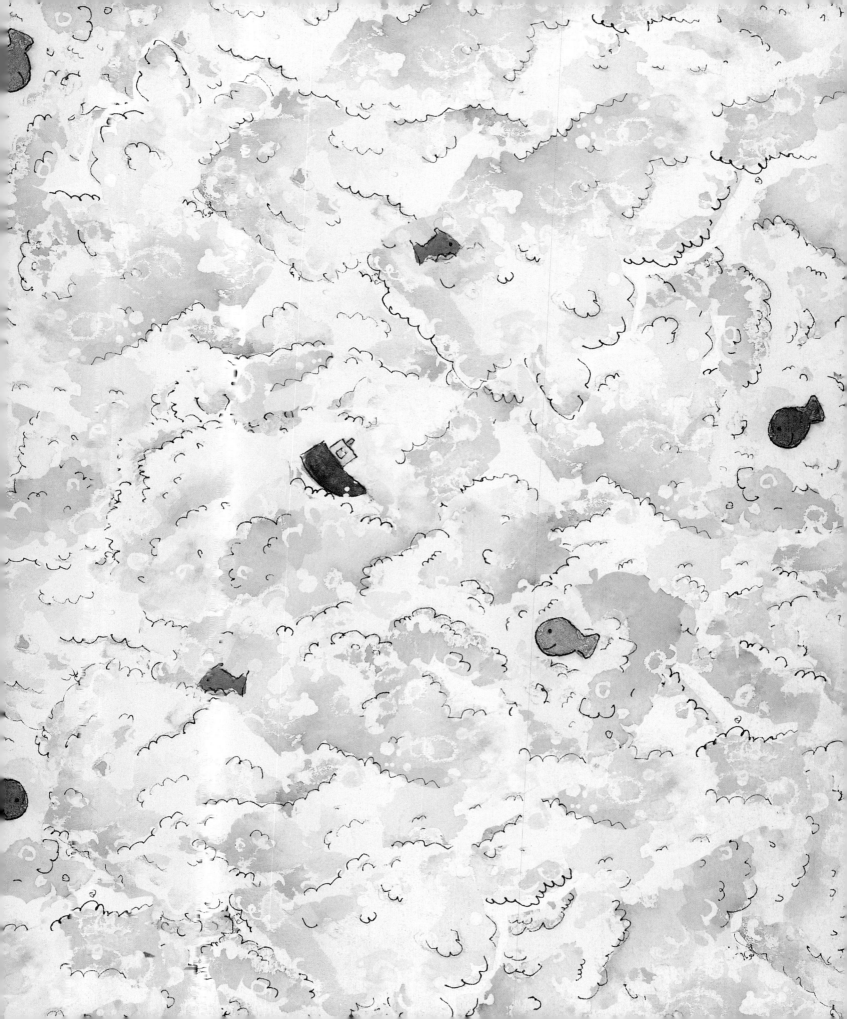